TO ROBIN
FOR GIVING ME A
BOTTOM LINE

Also by Tom Lang

coffee

"... *a deliciously satirical tale* ..."
    –The Oregonian
"**coffee** *romps through the highs and lows of the Northwest's favorite rocket fuel with sardonic speed ... nimble, savory prose* ..."
    —The Register-Guard

cat

"*Tom Lang's* **cat** *offers a deceptively deep and complex story in the guise of a simple tale about a reformed cat hater and his feline, Bouhaki. Lang paints his characters with deft strokes, sweetly hooking his unsuspecting reader's heart.*"
    —Shannon Brownlee, Senior Editor,
        U.S. News & World Report

eagle

"*Absolutely hilarious! By combining comedy with facts, Lang has created a unique and clever look at eagles and their private lives.*"
    —Nicole Duclos, Alaska Raptor Rehabilitation
        Center

mrs. claus

A Story by
Tom Lang

Published by BOUDELANG PRESS
Post Office Box 12379
Portland, OR 97212-0379
503.242.0870

Illustration and Concept by Andrew Reidenbaugh
Design by Siobhan Burns
Production by Sandy Hubbard

North Pole Consultant: Laurie Insley
Elf Help: Leland Zaitz and Marc Louria

Library of Congress Catalog Card Number 96-94888

ISBN 0-9649742-0-7

I WAS BORN TO RUN A FORTUNE 500 COMPANY. AT AGE 7 I owned, operated and franchised a chain of successful drive-through lemonade stands. In middle school I reengineered the cafeteria food lines to maximize playground time. As high school treasurer, I funneled "donations" through the principal's office to soften his views on independent study.

I went on to earn my MBA from a prestigious business school in the Midwest. For my master's thesis I evaluated the efficiency of my own school's business department. As a result of my recommendations, four

1

professors were denied tenure, two assistants were urged to "pursue other opportunities" and my advisor, an old friend of the family, was stripped of his pension.

Upon finishing my Workaholic in Residence Program at the local branch of the Foreclosure Bank of North America, I graduated at the top of my class. Recruiters fought over me as if I were a blue chip athlete. I chose a small-cap, high growth company with rapid multiple product introductions. Within months, with my solution-oriented instincts for problem solving, I became an invaluable member of the senior management team. However, after the first leg of my oxygen-depleting career arc, I found myself curiously unfulfilled.

I set a goal to get back on track. I hired a Chinese Feng Sui master to re-energize my office. Mr. Woo built a moat around my desk and filled it with exotic Oriental goldfish. He hung crystals from my ceiling and replaced my phone ringer with a ceremonial gong. I reread the #1 bestseller, "Rationalizations Seven Successful CEOs Use to Convince Themselves They're Doing Something Worthwhile

With Their Lives." I even refused to work more than 12 hours on Sundays.

Nothing helped. Was it me? Was it my job? Headhunters contacted me constantly, but I turned down lucrative offers every day. Then, one night, at 2 a.m., I turned in early. While flossing my teeth, checking my voice mail and balancing my check book, the business section fell off my lap onto the floor. I leaned out of bed and a block of letters from the page expanded in front of me:

> IMMEDIATE OPENING!!!!!
> Efficiency Expert at the North Pole
> Serious Inquiries Only

The North Pole! Now, that sounded interesting. I faxed my resume from the machine I kept on the nightstand next to my bed. I nodded to sleep and tiptoed into dreams. I skied across the white frosting of a gigantic birthday cake with lit candles the size of pine trees. I laughed and giggled until a horn went off in the wilderness. I stomped my feet and yelled for it to stop. I woke up to the sound of an incoming fax. I reached over, picked up the paper and turned on the light:

Would like to schedule an interview tomorrow night. Is midnight okay? My driver will pick you up. Dress warm.

Ho-ho-ho,

S.C.

To the amazement of the cleaning crew, I left work by 11 that night. I rushed home and changed into my blue wool power suit, assertive but friendly. I opened my laptop and reviewed my list of compensation requirements—short-term and long term bonus potential, transportation allowance, 401k, stock options, first-dollar medical and dental.

My computer scheduling program beeped. There was a thud at the door. It was midnight. I put the laptop in my briefcase, grabbed my coffee cup and stepped onto the porch of my condo. On the sidewalk stood 8 reindeer and a shiny, red sleigh, glowing like a hot coal.

"Wow, reindeer," I said, icicles racing down my extremities.

"Well, duh."

"Excuse me?" I said, looking around for the source of the voice. The reindeer in front of the pack turned to me.

"I said, 'Duh,' lady. What part of 'Duh' don't you understand?"

I dropped my briefcase, coffee spilled over my shoes.

"Talking reindeer."

"Double-Duh."

The other reindeer chuckled and stomped their hooves into the ground.

"You must be here to pick me up?" I said foolishly.

"No, lady, we were just in the neighborhood looking for our cousin Rudy and we thought you might be roasting him over an open fire."

The reindeer laughed, stomped and nudged each other with their antlers. They mumbled parts of the joke: ". . . just in the neighborhood . . . open fire . . . might be roasting . . ."

I checked my watch, straightened my suit, trying to act businesslike in front of 8 talking reindeer. I reached my hand out to the head reindeer.

"Hi, I'm—"

"Bob."

"Excuse me?"

"Name's Bob, ma'am. You have a problem with that?"

"No . . . uh . . . Bob is a lovely name . . . for a talking reindeer."

"Bob is a lovely name for a talking, flying reindeer, lady. Let's go."

I stepped up into the sleigh and grabbed hold of the reins, a feeling of wonder sizzling my skin. The reindeer shuffled their hooves and lifted off, the momentum plastering me to the seat. We rose above the trees, the houses and the high rise office buildings. We flew north, above a quilt of clouds, the stars blinding me like flashbulbs. Bob told stories while the reindeer joked and sang. I held on, the wind biting my face, spinning my hair into steel wool.

As we began our descent, the greens and reds of the Northern Lights danced in my head like a cartoon. We landed in the middle of the light show, on a snowed-in runway with a barely visible sign that read:

WELCOME TO THE NORTH POLE

SNOW FELL AROUND ME LIKE FEATHERS FROM A CELESTIAL pillow fight. I stepped out of the sleigh, took a breath and composed myself. Shoulders back, briefcase in hand, I trudged through the snow and opened the door to the complex. A voice yelled:

"Watch Out!"

An avalanche of clutter buried me in darkness, a bike pedal stuck in my ribs, a basketball flattening my ear. Somewhere out there a talking doll repeated, "I'm Patty, and I'm not afraid to say no."

I heard someone digging me out of my tomb.

A colander of light flowed through the spokes of a wheel pressed to my face. I looked up into a wall of red.

"Are you okay?"

"You're Santa Claus!" I said, as if he were an amnesia patient.

He nodded and helped me up. We were standing in a warehouse the size of an oceanliner. With the inventory system of my grandfather's garage, dolls, skis, clothes and games were stacked to the ceiling.

"Be right with you," Santa said, one hand full of crumbled papers, the other searching through the debris.

"Um, you lose something?"

"Not yet. Just can't find it right now," he said, looking up and shaking the papers at me. "Checking a list, you know."

Santa began excavating a corner, tossing packages and toys behind him like a dog digging a hole. He looked at me and shrugged. He walked over to a pair of rocking horses and sat on one, motioning for me to sit on the other.

"Things are a little disorganized right now," Santa said with a flip of his chubby hand and a nervous "Ho-ho-ho."

I rocked a few times, assembling my thoughts.

"This is your fulfillment center, I take it?"

"What's that?"

"This is where you fill your orders for gifts, right, Mr. Claus?"

"Uh, right."

"What type of database do you use?" I asked, rocking back and forth on my horsy.

"Database?"

"Database. How do you keep track? I mean, some years I get some pretty weird stuff, as if my list was crossed with somebody else's."

"Well, yeah, that happens once in a while," Santa said defensively.

"How do you control your inventory?"

"I check the list twice," he said with pride.

"That doesn't do much good if you're checking the wrong list, now does it?"

"Well . . ."

Santa looked around the room, down at the

papers in his hand.

"I'd like you to come in for a month or so and work out some of the glitches we've developed."

"A month or so?" I said, stopping my rocker. "I think you're underestimating the extent of your glitches, Mr. Claus."

"Nah, this is different than other businesses you deal with."

That's what they all say, I thought, as I reached for my laptop. Santa and I worked for an hour or two before he tired and went to bed. I stayed up and created spreadsheets and made to-do lists. Halfway through my personal brainstorming I eyed a pair of nearby rollerblades and couldn't resist the urge to lace them up. I skated around and around the warehouse floor until I collapsed, exhausted, in a heap of teddy bears, the images of reindeer dancing in my head.

"BAAAAATTER UP!"

The chatter of vowels jerked me awake. Funny looking children were jumping around me with frying pans in their hands. They tossed pancakes from one to another, singing gibberish about batter and syrup.

> "Put the heat up on the griddle
> Put the batter in the middle
> And flip those babies in the air"

I sat up. Wait a minute, I said to myself, looking at

the bells on their pointy shoes and their goofy little hats. It's the elves!

"Hey, what's going on here?" I said.

They turned to me and froze, flipped pancakes flopping on top of heads. The elves bounced over and introduced themselves. There was Flapjack and Griddlecake and Blintz and Chapatty and Crepe and Pfannekuchen and the Stack Brothers—One, Two and Three.

While they fed me breakfast (Swedish, German and apple pancakes) they told me their story. Raised in an orphanage run by a mean, black-balled short-order cook, they were fed only pancakes. One morning, during a grease fire in the kitchen, they escaped, and with the aid of Elf-Self-Help, a temporary elf employment agency, they found work at the North Pole. They took on batter related names, became gourmet flapjack chefs and constantly sang the classic ode to the pancake, "Batter Up."

I passed on a strawberry waffle and a blueberry blintz, my urge to work overcoming my hunger.

"What time do you boys have to be at work?"

"Whenever," they shrugged.

"What are you working on today?"

"Whatever," they shrugged.

"Hmmm," I said as I prepared for my 9 o'clock with Santa.

SANTA WAS LATE AND HIS OFFICE WAS A MESS, STACKED high with papers. I picked up a letter from the top of the pile and read it:

Dear Santa:

I'm not happy. You used to be nice but you don't give me the stuff I ask for anymore. Take me off your list and give my name to the Easter Bunny.

Georgia

Age 6

I read 20 more letters in the stack, all of them with the same complaints. Santa walked in, yawning and rubbing sleep from his eyes. I waved the letters at him.

"What happened to their gifts?"

"I don't know," he said, running his hands through his hair, "it happens once in a while."

"Define 'once in a while,' " I said, sweeping my hands over the reams of letters.

"Well . . ."

"Listen, Mr. Claus, it's only February and we have time to straighten things up around here. However, before I do anything, I need to ask your office manager a few questions."

"Office manager?"

I SENT A FAX TO MY OFFICE INFORMING THEM I WAS working off-site for a while. Then I began my evaluation of the work flow at the North Pole.

I sat down with the elves and had them describe their jobs to me. I asked them what their major complaints were and how we could resolve them. Although they mentioned shortage of raw materials, frantic, last minute production and various safety hazards in the workshop, they said they never viewed them as problems because that was the way it had always been. Bob and his crew felt the same way. Sure, there were flight delays and extended holding patterns, Bob said, but that was the price of doing business on Christmas Eve. Job satisfaction was rated high by all.

By the end of February a project scope was in place with timelines and milestones to help ease the December crunch. By March, with the elves pulling all-nighters with me, we had a complete stock inventory. In April the database was up and running, listing the gift receivees by region, age and gift request history. During May Bob and his herd and me and my stopwatch began our monthly practice runs, testing new routes and timing our deliveries.

Santa was impressed and pleased with the reorganization, but he showed little interest in learning about the business side of his operation. Not much of a head for it, he would say as he "Ho-ho-hoed" through the complex. However, I insisted upon giving him monthly slide presentations, weekly status reports and setting him down for a daily dinner meeting where I reviewed the day's events.

I eliminated 52 rework loops by June. Everyone had a copy of "From List to Delivery," a 750 page manual I threw together for reference points. There were T-shirts and posters on the walls that proclaimed our motto:

RIGHT LIST
RIGHT GIFT
RIGHT PERSON
RIGHT TIME

On Christmas Eve I gathered Santa and the elves in the living room. I wore the red dress and black boots the elves made for me.

"I want to thank everyone for all the hard work you put in to make the new changes—"

There was a bang on the window. Bob glared at us through the glass.

"Hey! Excuse me!" he yelled.

I ran to the door and opened it wide. The 8 of them tromped into the living room, knocking over furniture with their rumps, poking the elves into the air with their antlers.

"Hey! Watch it, Bobby!" Flapjack said, rubbing his bottom.

"Welcome," I said when the commotion died down.

"Nice to be invited, ma'am."

"Now, Bob, the Delivery Team Meeting isn't for ten minutes," I said, pointing to my watch, "you would know that if you'd read today's memos."

"Must have missed that one, ma'am. I could just kick myself."

"Save your strength, Bob, let me kick you."

The other reindeer laughed and butted antlers. I thanked everyone again, then handed out gifts— red nose warmers to the reindeer and real maple syrup to the elves. After our final checklist we were ready to hit the sleigh.

"Okay, you know the drill, let's go!"

With the precision of an Indy 500 pit crew, the elves funneled the sleigh with gifts and strapped harnesses on the reindeer. Santa jumped in the driver's seat and grabbed the reins. I sat beside him, my laptop loaded with the list database in one hand, a folder with indexed maps in the other. I reached my hand out to Santa.

"Ready, Mr. Claus?"

"Ready," Santa said, shaking my hand. "On Bob."

The reindeer pulled hard, jerking the sleigh forward like a railroad car. We lifted off, circled around the complex and headed south, the wind at our backs. Bob and Santa bantered back and forth, telling stories of Christmas past. We stopped at small houses and large houses, at hospitals and orphanages, wherever there were children who needed toys.

I kept an eye on the time as I checked the list twice. I fed the crew Reindeer Power Enhancement Bars when their energy levels dipped. I was all business and this was my watch. When we hit Haines, Alaska, one of our last stops, a heat surged through me. The snow covered rooftops and the Christmas trees in the windows made me clap my hands and hug myself in delight. It was Christmas Eve night and I was riding along in Santa's sleigh!

"Ho-ho-ho, Merry Christmas," Santa said as we landed on the air strip back at the Pole.

"Merry Christmas to you, Mr. Claus," I said, checking my watch and making one last entry in my computer.

We sat silently in the sleigh, toasted by the glow of giving, watching the falling snow cleanse the night. I looked over at Santa and for the first time, I thought—you know, he's kind of cute.

"ARE YOU SEEING ANYONE?"

"Sort of."

"I thought so. You don't call for almost a year. A year! I have to call your office to find out you've quit your high-paying, high-profile job and moved to Northern Poland."

"No, mother, not Northern—"

"So, what does he do?"

"He works with underprivileged children and—"

"There's no money in that."

"It's non-profit, mother."

"There is plenty of money in non-profit, dear. A CEO can make a bundle—bonus, compensation, padded expense accounts. You just have to keep it quiet."

"Please, mother—"

"I'll plan on you two coming for Christmas this year."

"That's not a good time for us, Mother."

"You owe me that much, don't you think, for all I've done for you?"

"Well, okay, but we can only stay for a second."

I NEVER CONSIDERED THE CHANCE OF ROMANCE IN ANY work environment, let alone the North Pole. After our first Christmas success, Santa wanted to take a few weeks off, but I insisted we get back to work bright and early on December 26th. There was much to do and I stressed to Santa that he had much to learn about running a successful company.

As we continued to work together, I felt the heat of proximity. Something was melting at the North Pole, and it wasn't from global warming. Whether it was his beard tickling my arm as I handed him a graph or when I would squeeze by his soft, round belly on my way to the printer, there was the tingle of love at the North Pole.

I denied the feelings at first. He was my boss, for goodness sake. How many articles in women's magazines had I read about this very peril? Then there was the age issue. I didn't know how old he was, but he was at least as old as my mother.

I could tell Santa had similar feelings for me. I caught him staring at me while I prepared spreadsheets and work tasks. He would look away, turn redder than usual, and give a self-conscious "Ho-ho-ho."

We took walks out in the snow while I taught him about process mapping, reengineering and rework loops. One day I slipped on the ice and he caught me and held me tight.

"Are you okay?"

"Yes, thank you, Mr. Claus," I said, resting my head on his chest.

"Call me Santa," he said.

We stood there, the wind frisking us, Santa's heart pounding in my ear. Goodness radiated from somewhere deep inside his girth, a spot I had never found within myself. Where I came from people gave in order to control others, their apparent generosity really a chit to be cashed in at an opportune time. But Santa had a purity of heart that flowed into me like a blood transfusion.

We married a few months later during a blizzard in front of the workshop. Bob, who became an ordained minister through a number he found in the back of Reindeer Journal, performed the ceremony. The reindeer sang and danced while the elves threw dollar pancakes.

We didn't have time for a honeymoon, I told Santa, but maybe next year. There was too much work to be done. My pro-active production plan was a week behind schedule, the number of flight delays was unacceptable and the stopover time ratio made me toss and turn all night.

The next year, during the first week of December, right on schedule, I had a baby boy, Sammy. Sandy came along a year later. I told Santa it was time for me to take one step back from the business and for him to take one step forward. With confidence in my system, I stayed home with the kids on Christmas Eve.

And life was good.

For his fourth birthday Santa gave Sammy a miniature chimney with real soot. At five, he gave our son a sleighcycle with voice-activated stuffed reindeer. By six, Sammy was putting on weight and "Ho-ho-hoing" around the house.

As a child, Sandy rode on her daddy's shoulders while Santa went about preparing for Christmas. "List" was one of the first words she learned after "Mama," "Dada," and "Bob." The elves' workshop was my own little day care center for her. Sandy loved sitting with Flapjack at his workbench, laughing and clapping, eating hotcakes and singing along to "Batter Up."

Yes, life was good.

"DAD, CAN I DRIVE THE SLEIGH THIS YEAR?"

"Not this year, Sammy. Maybe next year."

"You say that every year."

"Do I? Well, not this Christmas. Maybe next year."

"Then can we finally go to Hawaii for a vacation?"

"This year is too busy. Maybe next year."

"I'm going to be 12 next week. All I ask for every Christmas is for you to take me to Hawaii."

"We don't give you great gifts?"

"Yeah, everything but what I want."

"So, why don't you and Bob go? He'd love it."

"Bob? Dad, I want to go with you. That's the point."

"Maybe next year."

"Let's talk about this after dinner," I said

"Not tonight, dear," Santa said, "I have to work late at the shop."

Sammy, head down, poked his food with his fork, staring at his pasta as if it were a pile of worms.

THINGS WERE CHANGING AT THE NORTH POLE. AT FIRST I
thought it was all for the good. Santa took my
advice and became active in the nuts and bolts of
the company. He drilled me on basic business the-
ories and subscribed to 25 business magazines,
from *Business Week* to *Downsizer* to *Loopholes
Monthly*. He read every column in the *Wall Street
Journal* except the editorials.

Driven by his new knowledge, he realized the
department store process arc from Halloween
to Christmas Day was too small a window of

opportunity. Santa hit the road year round promoting his image on talk shows, at Pro-Mythological golf tournaments and summer camps for future street corner Santas. He sponsored a professional wrestling extravaganza—the Battle of the Department Store Santas.

It all appeared to be working so well. The number of letters from disgruntled children dwindled. Santa was more popular than ever, immortalized in new songs and hit movies, buried in an avalanche of fan mail. He was voted "Sexiest Man Alive" for an unprecedented three years in a row.

But the more time he spent with the world, the less time he spent with his family. Sammy, now in his teens, withdrew, watched his weight and went on week-long juice fasts. Sandy rebelled, turning her room into a shambles, refusing to use the index system I designed for her closet. She immersed herself in the teachings of obscure pagan religions.

Then the layoffs began.

"LET ME GET THIS STRAIGHT, FAT MAN. YOU'RE SHUFFLING me and the crew out to the back 40 for some kind of spacecraft?"

"Hovercraft, Bob."

"Oh, hovercraft. Well, excuse me and my big ignorant rump."

Bob and Santa never argued. I could see and hear them through the window as they stood outside the complex, the falling snow bleaching them into the backdrop.

"Let me ask you this, Santa baby. Have me and my

crew ever missed any deliveries?"

"No, of course not."

"Have we ever been late on our rounds?"

"No."

"So, everything's fine. Well, it must be time to send the boys to the sausage factory."

"Early retirement, Bob."

"Early retirement. Well, it's too early to retire. We love our job. And you're not the only star around here. They write songs about us, too. 'Here comes Santa and his hovercraft' is not what I would call a catchy hook."

"Bob, this move is for technological advancement. I think you'll see this is best for the company."

"Best for the company? How many years have we broken our backs hauling your fat butt all over the world? And you're telling me what's best for the company doesn't include us?"

"You're not looking at the big picture, Bob."

"Oh, yeah, well I've got a big picture for you right here, fat man."

Bob turned around and wiggled his rump in Santa's face, then stomped through the snow to the stable. Yes, things were changing at the North Pole.

"WE'RE LIMITING OUR RESOURCE ALLOCATION TO STRENGTH-en our core business."

"Wow, cool, Santa."

I was standing outside the office. I recognized Flapjack's voice through the door.

"As a valued member of our transition team, we would like to offer you an incentive to relocate."

"Relocate?"

"Yes."

"Leave the North Pole?"

"Yes, Flapjack. Next year we will be outsourcing

our production to some cost-saving labor markets. We need you to relocate as a consultant."

"But this is my home, Santa. All my friends are here. I don't know anybody outside of here."

"This is a terrific vertical move for you, Flapjack."

"But I'm happy right here. I don't want to go."

"There's no longer a job for you here. There is a job for you down there."

The door opened and Flapjack, his head down, shuffled by me. I stepped inside the office. Santa beamed and opened his arms.

"Isn't this great, honey?" he said. "I do have a knack for this side of the business."

Santa kissed and hugged me tight, squeezing the breath out of me.

"I owe it all to you, honey."

ON HIS 18TH BIRTHDAY, SAMMY MOVED AWAY FROM THE
North Pole. He was now a thin, gaunt young man,
withdrawn and sullen. He seldom laughed. He
bummed a ride off of Bob, who was more than
happy to fly him to Hawaii where Sammy went
into retail.

Four months later, Sandy, distraught over the
relocation of Flapjack, ran away from home. She
joined a cult that neither exchanged gifts nor cele-
brated holidays. Her sect believed that rodents
were re-incarnated holymen and Sandy founded

Creatures Are Stirring, a solidarity group for mice. She changed her birthday to February 2, Ground-hog Day.

Santa minimized the impact of their departure.

"They're kids, honey, it's a phase. Look, I think I've figured out a drop shipment system that will cut some fat off our payroll."

The next few Christmas Eves I spent alone, sitting in my rocking chair, the house smothered in silence. Santa was out in the hovercraft, with its Global Positioning System and automatic list checker. How did it come to this, I thought, as my head nodded up and down, in and out of sleep, memory tugging at me like a puppet string. After all my work, how did I end up all alone, with no friends or family, just like I was before I came to the North Pole?

Then, on one more lonely Christmas Eve, with a draft biting my ankles and my rocker creaking a sad tune, Griddlecake ran into the room.

"Mrs. Claus, Flapjack has disappeared."

I sat up, shook my head, leaned forward.

"I just got a call from the factory down south,"

Griddlecake said. "Flapjack didn't show up for work today, Mrs. Claus. He wouldn't do that on the busiest day of the year."

My mind was clearing, my head buzzing, a jar full of bees.

"What are we going to do, Mrs. Claus? He must be in trouble."

I reached over and hugged Griddlecake.

"I'll go find him and bring him home."

I stood up, moving with instinct, vision and purpose. I went to the closet and put on my old red dress It must have shrunk, I thought as I bent over and pulled on my black boots. I made my way across to the reindeer stable and opened the door. A wave of snow surfed in on the wind. "Bob," I said, "let's ride."

THE SLEIGH WAS RUSTY, THE PAINT FADED. BOB AND HIS CREW had grown thick around the middle and the elves had to expand the harness straps to make them fit.

"Where we headed, Mrs. C?" Bob asked, pumped for action.

"South, Bob."

"Let's do it boys."

We took off into a headwind and fought our way across the latitudes. We landed somewhere in the Yukon. Bob and his crew huffed and puffed.

"Is there a problem?" I asked.

"Uh . . . (cough, heave) . . . nothing, Mrs. C."

"You boys a little winded?"

"Us . . . (hack) . . . no way. Never felt better. Right fellas?"

The other 7 reindeer nodded as they coughed and sputtered.

". . . you got that right . . . top of our game . . . feel great. . . ."

After a brief rest we continued south to the state of Washington. Bob stopped for a break on Mt. Rainier, then we flew over Mt. Saint Helen's, down the Columbia River and up the Willamette River to Northeast Portland. I found the address I wanted on 10th Avenue.

I walked up the stairs and knocked on the door. An army of tiny feet tap danced away as a pair of big feet marched toward me. A curtain parted, a doorknob turned. Sandy poked her head through the opening.

"Mom. What are you doing here?"

"I need your help. Let me in."

Sandy didn't move, her face scrunched up as if focusing on a complicated math equation.

"Sandy Claus, open this door, NOW!" I said, stomping my boot on the porch.

Startled, she stepped back and I walked past her. An altar with cheese and treadmills stood in the center of the candle-lit living room. Mice scampered back and forth.

"This place is a mess. Grab your coat, I need your help."

"I can't leave, Mom," Sandra said in a hushed tone. "I have a duty and responsibility here. Do you know who these mice are? They're reincarnated holymen, and I'm their sworn protector."

Sandy pointed around the room.

"This is Krishna, and Buddha, Mohammed, this is Moses, and geez, Gandhi is around here somewhere."

"That's very nice, dear, but we have to go."

"Mom—"

"Sandy, get your coat. I need your help. You owe me this."

"Owe you, Mom? Is that what giving's about? The more you give, the more you're owed?"

My mother's voice echoed in my head and a

sharp pain from childhood burrowed into my stomach. I closed my eyes and focused on my mission.

"We have to go, NOW!" I said, stomping my boot again. I felt a squish under my heel, heard a pop like a walnut in a nutcracker. Sandy and I looked down at my boot. She bent over.

"Oh, no, Mom, it's Gandhi. He doesn't look good."

"I'm sorry, honey, but he'll be back . . . someday."

She held the mouse in her hands like a chalice.

"Honey, Flapjack is missing from his post."

Sandra looked up at me, her eyes wide, the elf's name a Pavlovian trigger to her childhood. She dropped the dead mouse on the floor.

"Missing? What does that mean?"

"I don't know. That's why we have to hurry. NOW!"

"Watch where you step, Mom! I'm coming."

I held the door open for Sandy while I watched Moses and Mohammed spinning on their treadmills.

WHILE SANDY HUGGED THE REINDEER, I JUMPED BACK IN THE driver's seat and we headed west, the wind raking us with needles of rain. Bob and his herd slid into a groove, singing and joking like old times. The weather cleared when we turned south over the Pacific Ocean.

Stars twinkled and whales breeched as we approached the island of Maui. We landed on the main street of Paia, the last address I had for Sammy. The stores lining the street stood wrapped in Christmas decorations and draped in banners of

45

holiday cheer. My son's shop sat at the end of the block, its black-striped candy cane neon sign blinking: THE ANTI-CHRISTMAS STORE. As we approached Sammy stormed out of the storefront and chased away a group of Christmas carolers.

"And Merry Christmas to you," I said.

He whirled around like a gunfighter. Recognition softened his face.

"Mom . . . Sandy . . . Bob?"

"How's business, son?"

"Oh, a little slow," he said, defensively, sounding like his father.

"Imagine that."

"Very funny, Mom," he said.

"Flapjack is missing, son, and you can help us find him."

"Why should I? So you can send him back to that awful factory?"

"We're taking him back to the North Pole, where he belongs, where we all belong."

"I don't belong there."

"We don't have time for this, son. Come with us."

"I can't help you, Mom."

Bob reared up on his hind legs, pulling at the harness like a bull in a stall.

"Don't you talk to your mother like that, boy! Let me at him!"

Bob dragged the rest of the team toward the building and pinned Sammy against the wall with his antlers.

"Get your butt in this sleigh right now or I will stick these antlers in your behind and drag you with us. What'll be, Sammy Boy?"

"Okay, Bob, okay, but I'm not staying at the North Pole."

"Who would want you around with that attitude. Now, get in the sleigh."

Sammy climbed into the back of the sleigh and slumped into the corner. I looked over at Bob, but he looked away.

SANDY TOLD US TO FLY TO CALIFORNIA. IN HIS LETTERS, SHE said, Flapjack told her Venice Beach was the only place he seemed to fit in. We zoomed across the ocean and landed near the Venice Pier.

"Where do we start?" I asked Sandy.

"He said he sings in a bar around here," she said.

"That should be easy to find," Bob snorted, "he only knows one song."

We walked down the strand, Sammy sulking behind us. We showed Flapjack's picture to street corner Santas as they roller-skated by, but they only shook their beards. We turned down a street lined with restaurants and bars. Through the wall of holiday music flowing from the buildings, we heard the strains of an old familiar song. Sandy grabbed my arm as a raucous chorus of "Batter Up" roared from inside a biker bar across the street.

"Look!" Sandy yelled.

Flapjack, with bells on his slippers and his little elf hat on his head, stumbled out of the bar, through a row of motorcycles and dropped to his knees over a sewer drain.

"Flapjack!" we all said as we ran to him.

"Mrs. C., Sandy, Sammy . . . Oh, I don't feel so good."

Flapjack put his head down, recycling a meal into the gutter. I leaned over him, the smell of liquor sucking the air out of my lungs.

"Flapjack, you're drunk. You don't drink."

"But I'm unhappy, Mrs. C."

"Getting drunk doesn't help, Flapjack."

"It doesn't? But that's what unhappy people do down here. Boy, am I sick."

"Come on, Flapjack, we're taking you home."

"I don't have a home anymore."

"Yes, you do. We're taking you back to the North Pole."

"I'll be good, I swear I will."

"You were never bad, Flapjack."

"I must have done something terrible to make Santa send me away, Mrs. C."

I picked Flapjack up and hugged him, my mind muddled with emotions. A huge, bearded man dressed in leather walked out of the bar and started up his motorcycle. He noticed Flapjack and pointed his finger at us.

"Hey, little dude, the pancake song rocks."

SANDY HELD FLAPJACK'S HEAD OVER THE SIDE OF THE SLEIGH as Bob guided us north over the old delivery route we had honed so many years before. Above Haines, the necklace of lights rimming the small boat harbor triggered memories of my first Christmas run with Santa and the dull ache of the past swept over me. Flapjack perked up, as if from a cattle prod.

"Down there!" he yelled. "It's Santa!"

Santa lay sprawled in the snow, gifts scattered around him like confetti. The hovercraft sat smashed into a building in the middle of the parade grounds.

We landed and the four of us rushed to his side.

"Santa, are you okay?" I said, my heart exploding, "what happened?"

"Oh, my leg," he moaned, dazed by shock. "Darn machine doesn't listen to me like Bob did." Santa chuckled a weak "Ho-ho-ho."

"It's not broken, honey," I said after I squeezed my hands down his leg. I checked my watch. "The deliveries are way behind schedule. Let's use the sleigh."

The kids and Flapjack gathered the gifts and loaded the sleigh. We huffed, puffed and grunted to get Santa on his feet but when I watched him hobble I knew he was in no shape to chimney hop. Santa tried to slide into the driver's seat, but Sammy stopped him.

"Get in the back, Dad."

"I'm driving, Sammy."

"You've already wrecked one vehicle. Get in the back and relax. I'm driving."

"This is my sleigh. I'm driving."

"Not now you're not. But," Sammy said, pausing for effect, "maybe next year."

Santa stared at our son, frowned, then nodded in revelation. We helped him into the back seat and I sat beside him, keeping his leg elevated. Just as Sammy grabbed the reins, Flapjack turned to me.

"We don't have a list, Mrs. Claus."

"Oh, yes, we do," I said, reaching under the seat for my laptop and turning it on. I squinted at the blur on the screen, feeling through my pockets for my glasses. Sandy snatched the computer from my lap.

"I'll handle this, Mom. You take care of Dad."

"On Bob," Sammy said as we taxied along the snow and up into the night. I sat back, Santa's head in my lap, and watched our children work. Sandy checked the list while Flapjack refilled the sack between stops. Sammy, with the fervor of a firefighter, slid up and down the chimneys. With speed, enthusiasm and teamwork they finished ahead of schedule.

"This is Big Red to base," Sandy said into the radio, "do you copy?"

"This is base," Griddlecake's voice scratched through the air.

"We've got Flapjack and we're coming home."

"That boy can drive a sleigh," Bob said as we landed

back at the Pole, the Northern Lights blazing like a Mardi Gras party. Griddlecake and the gang raced out of the complex, hugging Flapjack and Sandy and freeing the reindeer. Blintz and Chapatty ran back inside to get a stretcher for Santa while the reindeer danced and slapped antlers in celebration of their trip.

The purity and joy of the moment bathed me in light. I looked down at Santa and took his hand. He looked over at Sammy who was standing in front of the sleigh, staring at the complex.

"Nice job, son," Santa said.

Sammy nodded and walked away. I squeezed Santa's hand and stroked his head.

"Let's talk, Santa," I said.

An hour later we gathered for breakfast in the dining room. Bob had everyone in hysterics, telling jokes, doing impressions, reliving the night's highlights. Pancakes sat on the table, piled high like a stack of poker chips. I tapped on a gallon jug of maple syrup.

"I want to welcome Flapjack back to the North Pole," I said.

Applause, hooting, tossing of pancakes.

"And I also want to thank Sandy and Sammy for

visiting us."

More applause, stomping of hooves, slapping of antlers.

"Santa and I have been talking and we've made a few decisions. First, if Bob and the crew agree, Santa wants them back as his delivery team next year."

"Early retirement for the hovercraft!" Bob said, raising a hoof in the air.

"Second, we are returning to our centralized production system, which means we need you back, Flapjack."

"Yes!" the elves said, exploding from their seats like sports fans.

While I watched the reindeer dance on tables and listened to the elves sing "Batter Up," I thought about my life at the North Pole. What a success I had been at efficiency, but what a failure I was at effectiveness. How many times had I towed the bottom line of low cost production when the real bottom line was celebrating right before me.

"Mom, are you okay?"

I shook my head and turned toward Sandy, who was swing dancing with Bob.

"Pardon me, honey?"

"I said, 'Are you okay?' You're staring."

"Oh, I'm fine, sweetheart."

Sandy rushed over and hugged me, squeezing me tight.

"I love you, Mom."

Bob stepped up and gave me a wet, slobbering kiss, his breath stinging my eyes. I mopped my cheek with my sleeve.

"I love you, too, Mrs. C."

The elves and the other reindeer rushed to me, kissing and hugging me as if I'd scored a winning soccer goal. Sammy fought through the crowd and whispered in my ear.

"Merry Christmas, Mom," he said.

My throat was tight, my skin massaged by electricity. I grabbed Santa's hand so I wouldn't float away. I made a goal to get back on track, but this plan came from my heart, not my head. What was good for me would be good for our family, and what was good for our family would be good for our company, and what was good for our company would be good for the world.

Now that's a bottom line I could live with.

BOUDELANG PRESS ORDER FORM

Name_____

Street_____

City_____State_____Zip_____

Add $1 for shipping on individual book orders. For 3 or more books, add a flat $3.

Please send the following:

	mrs. claus				TOTAL
Quantity	_____			x $7 = _____

	coffee	cat	eagle		
Quantity	_____	____	_____	x $5 = _____

Shipping   + _____

                                        TOTAL DUE = _____

Please make checks payable to : BOUDELANG PRESS
                                                P.O. BOX 12379
                                                Portland, OR 97212-0379

Questions? Please call: 503.242.0870